A Just Right Book

Baby Night Owl

By Leslie McGuire
Illustrated by Mary Szilagyi

Random House New York

It was morning. Baby Night Owl yawned a great big yawn.

"The sun is coming up," said Mama Night Owl. "It's time for little night owls to go to bed."

Baby Night Owl did not want to go to bed. He stuck out his feathers.

"No," he said. "I'm not sleepy."

"Don't be silly," said Mama Night Owl. "Come snuggle down in the nest. I'll sing you a song."

"No," said Baby Night Owl. "I want to stay up. I want to see the day."

"There is nothing to see during the day," said Mama Night Owl. "Everything that is interesting is sleeping. Mice sleep during the day. Moths sleep during the day. Bats sleep during the day. And so do baby night owls."

Baby Night Owl looked outside. The sky was pink. Day was coming. But his mama was starting to sing. She sang about silvery shadows, and delicious pale-green moths, and twinkling stars, and the large shiny moon.

She sang about all the things in the night. It was
such a nice song that soon Mama Night Owl
closed her eyes and fell asleep. But Baby Night Owl
was still awake.

Baby Night Owl hopped out of the nest and onto a branch of the hollow tree. He blinked his eyes. It was very bright outside. The sun was like a big yellow eye in the sky. It was brighter than a hundred moons.

Baby Night Owl blinked again. There were so many colors. Everything was red and yellow and pink and blue and green and orange. Flowers lay across the meadow like a rainbow. At night the meadow always looked like a carpet of soft silvery feathers.

And it was noisy. Instead of the quiet hush of night, there were all kinds of sounds. Birds were singing in the trees. Bees were buzzing in the flowers. Grasshoppers were chirping in the tall grass.

Suddenly Baby Night Owl saw a long fluffy tail flick past the end of a branch. The tail stopped, and he saw that it was attached to a furry animal. The furry animal turned around.

"What are you?" asked the furry animal.

"I am a night owl," answered Baby Night Owl, blinking. "What are you?"

"I am a squirrel," said the squirrel.

"Why aren't you asleep?" asked Baby Night Owl.

"I sleep at night," said the squirrel. "Don't you know anything?"

Baby Night Owl stuck out his feathers. He said, "I know a lot of things. I know all about the night."

"That's silly. There is nothing to know about the night," said the squirrel. "Everything that is interesting is asleep at night."

"That's not true," said Baby Night Owl. He thought for a minute. Then he said, "I'll tell you about the night if you'll tell me about the day."

Baby Night Owl listened as the squirrel told him the names of everything in the meadow.

"Cow," the squirrel said, pointing to a big thing.
"Dog," he said, pointing to a noisy thing.

It was so bright in the meadow, Baby Night Owl had a hard time keeping his eyes open. There was so much barking and mooing and buzzing and chirping that Baby Night Owl had a hard time remembering everything the squirrel said.

Baby Night Owl got all mixed up.

"Dogs say *moo*," he said to the squirrel. "Cows say *woof*."

The squirrel laughed at him. "Dogs say *woof*, silly. Cows say *moo*. Isn't day interesting?"

"Yes," Baby Night Owl told the squirrel. "But night is better." And then Baby Night Owl told the squirrel everything about the night.

"There are silvery shadows, and delicious pale-green moths, and twinkling stars, and a large shiny moon," he said.

The squirrel nibbled on a seed as he listened.
"Isn't night interesting?" said Baby Night Owl.

"Yes, but day is better. Day is busy and noisy and colorful," said the squirrel.

"Night is quiet and peaceful and beautiful," said Baby Night Owl.

Suddenly Baby Night Owl heard a rustling behind him. It was Mama Night Owl. She had one eye open.

"I have to go to bed," said Baby Night Owl.

"I have to find more seeds," said the squirrel. He flicked his long fluffy tail and ran down the side of the hollow tree. Baby Night Owl fluffed his feathers and hopped back into the nest.

"What are you doing?" asked Mama Night Owl.

"I saw the day," said Baby Night Owl.

Mama Night Owl opened both her eyes. "Tell me what you saw."

Baby Night Owl snuggled up against his mama.

"There are loud noises and so many colors," he said. "There are big animals, and the sun is as bright as a hundred moons. But night is better."

Then Mama Night Owl sang him the song about the night. She sang about the silvery shadows, and the twinkling stars, and the delicious pale-green moths.

When Baby Night Owl was almost asleep, his mama said, "Day sounds very nice. Why do you think night is better?"

Baby Night Owl gave a great big yawn and said, "Night is better because that's when my mama is awake. I love you, Mama."

"I love you, too," said his mama. "You are the sweetest little night owl in the forest."

Then Baby Night Owl snuggled into the nest and fell fast asleep.

Library of Congress Cataloging-in-Publication Data:
McGuire, Leslie. Baby Night Owl. (A Just right book) SUMMARY: A baby night owl stays awake to see what the daytime is like and has a discussion with a squirrel about whether day is better than night.   ISBN: 0-394-89986-5 (trade); 0-394-99986-X (lib. bdg.)   [1. Owls—Fiction. 2. Day—Fiction. 3. Night—Fiction] I. Szilagyi, Mary, ill. II. Title. III. Series: Just right book (New York, N.Y.)
PZ7.M4786Bab   1989   [E]   88-43033

Manufactured in the United States of America   1 2 3 4 5 6 7 8 9 10

JUST RIGHT BOOKS is a trademark of Random House, Inc.